I can move

First published in the U.S. in 1992 by Carolrhoda Books, Inc.

This edition published by special arrangement with
Carolrhoda Books, Inc., Minneapolis, MN. All rights reserved.

Copyright © 1991 Firefly Books Ltd., Hove, East Sussex.
First published 1991 Firefly Books Ltd.

Library of Congress Cataloging-in-Publication Data
Suhr, Mandy.
    I can move / by Mandy Suhr; illustrated by Mike Gordon.
        p. cm. - (I'm alive)
    Summary: Explains how our bones and muscles help our
body move.
    ISBN 0-87614-735-X (lib. bdg.)
    1. Musculoskeletal system - Juvenile literature. [1. Skeleton.
2. Bones. 3. Muscles.] I. Gordon, Mike, ill. II. Title.
III. Series: Suhr, Mandy. I'm alive.
QM100.S84 1992
611'.7-dc20   91-30561
                                                         CIP
                                                          AC

Printed in U.S.A.

1   2   3   4   5   6   7   8   9   10   01   00   99   98   97   96   95   94   93   92

I can move

written by Mandy Suhr

illustrated by Mike Gordon

I'm alive!

Carolrhoda Books, Inc./Minneapolis

When I was born,
I was very
little.

I could kick my feet
and move my arms,
but I couldn't
even sit up.

I had to be carried everywhere.

As I grew, my bones
and muscles got bigger
and stronger,

and soon I could move
around on my own.

I can move in lots of different ways now.

I can skip,

run,

jump,

roll, and dance.

I can do all these things because
I have a skeleton inside my body.

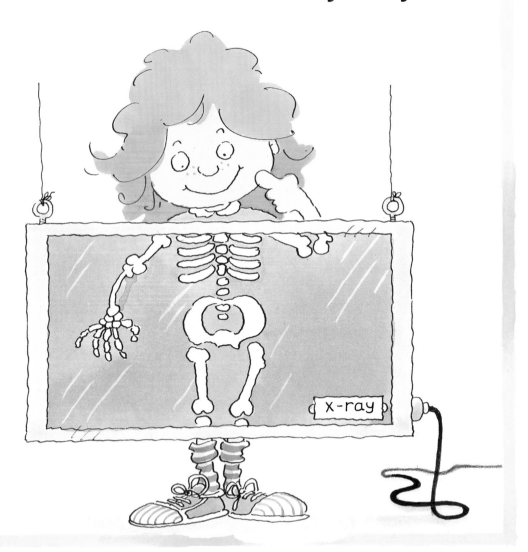

If I didn't have one, I wouldn't be able to stand up. I'd be all floppy!

Our skeletons are made up of
lots of different bones–big bones
and small bones all joined together.

Bones are very hard and
very strong. They don't
bend easily.

But we need to bend to move.
It is the joined parts
of our skeletons
that move.

My knees and
elbows bend
where two
bones join
together.

So do my fingers . . .

and my toes.

This is my backbone.

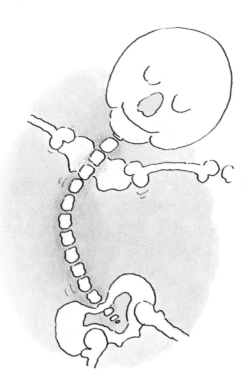

It's really lots of small bones
joined together, so it bends.

My backbone goes all the way
from my head, down my back,
to my bottom.

Muscles make my bones move.

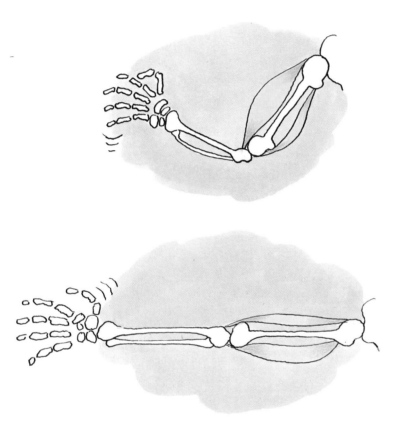

They are like big stretchy rubber bands attached to the bones.

My muscles pull the bones up and
down when I move.

Lots of animals have skeletons
as we do.

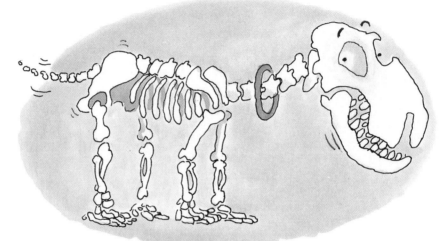

This is my dog, Jess.

This is my
goldfish, Jaws.

Birds have skeletons too.

This skeleton is just like the one inside you and me.

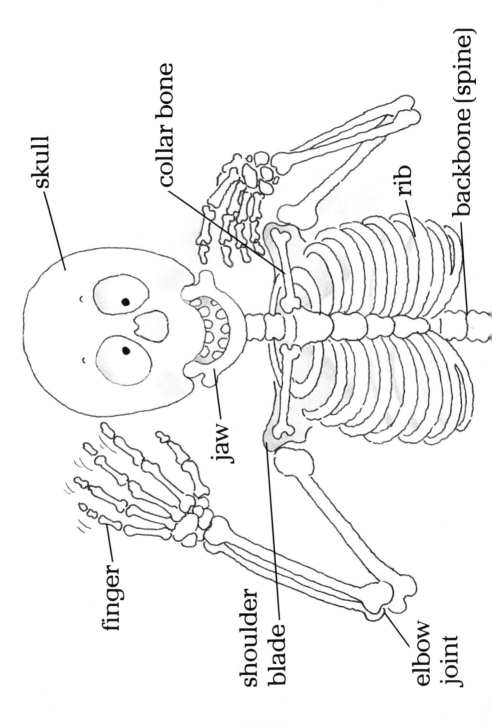

skull

collar bone

rib

backbone (spine)

jaw

finger

shoulder blade

elbow joint

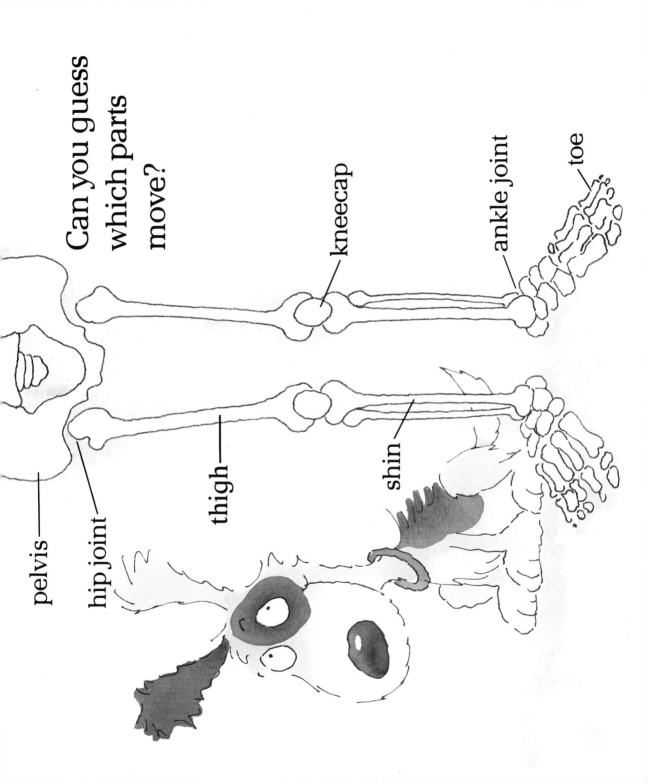

Can you guess which parts move?

pelvis

hip joint

thigh

kneecap

shin

ankle joint

toe

A note to adults

"I'm Alive" is a series of books designed especially for preschoolers and beginning readers. These books look at how the human body works and develops. They compare the human body to plants and animals that are already familiar to children.

Here are some activities that use what kids already know to help them learn more about how we move.

Activities

1. Make a poster that shows the different ways you can move your body. Find pictures of people dancing, running, crawling, sitting, walking, or make your own drawings. Cut out pictures from magazines or newspapers. Paste them to your poster.

2. Put one hand around the upper part of your arm. Now bend and straighten your arm. Can you feel your muscles getting fatter and thinner as they move? Can you feel the bones bend at your elbow? What other muscles can you feel?

3. Count the places that can bend in one of your hands. How many places did you find? Is this the same number that your brother or sister or friend found? Now try counting the places that bend in one foot.

4. People move in different ways. Some people use wheelchairs or crutches to help them move. What would it be like to use a wheelchair or crutches in your house or school? Can you find the places, like stairs, where it would be hard to move?